BY STEPHANIE CALMENSON   ILLUSTRATED BY BAPTISTE AMSALLEM

SIMON SPOTLIGHT

An imprint of Simon & Schuster Children's Publishing Division
New York   London   Toronto   Syndey   New Delhi
1230 Avenue of the Americas, New York, New York 10020 • This Simon Spotlight edition
September 2022 • Text copyright © 2022 by Stephanie Calmenson • Illustrations copyright ©
2022 by Baptiste Amsallem. All rights reserved, including the right of reproduction in whole
or in part in any form. SIMON SPOTLIGHT, READY-TO-READ, and colophon are registered
trademarks of Simon & Schuster, Inc. For information about special discounts for bulk
purchases, please contact Simon & Schuster Special Sales at 1-866-506-1949 or
business@simonandschuster.com. • Manufactured in the United States of America 0822 LAK
10 9 8 7 6 5 4 3 2 1 • This book has been cataloged with the Library of Congress.
ISBN 978-1-6659-1659-2 (hc) • ISBN 978-1-6659-1658-5 (pbk) • ISBN 978-1-6659-1660-8 (ebook)

Here is a list of the words you will find in this story. You might like to sound them out before you begin reading.

Names:

Zak   Ziggy

Word families:

"-ad"	→	bad	mad
"-at"	→	flat	that
"-ike"	→	bike	hike
"-out"	→	out	shout
"-un"	→	fun	run
"-us"	→	bus	us

Sight words:

a	again	am	did	do
feet	follow	for	from	go
here	I	in	is	it
look	my	no	not	on
one	ride	show	the	there
this	time	to	want	we
what	where	will	yes	you

Bonus words:

afraid	beat	being	breathe	cannot
comes	count	everyone	hang	happy
has	hear	hooray	join	late
miss	party	room	slowly	stomp
ten	tire	train	very	wait

Ready to go? Happy reading!

Don't miss the questions about the story
on the last page of this book.

The train is late.

We cannot wait.

Here comes a bus.

It has no
room for us.

There is no time
to hike.

We will ride
a bike.

Did you hear that?

The tire is flat!

Being late is no fun.

Hang on, Zak!
We will run!

I am afraid we will
miss the show!

NO!!!
This is very bad.

I am very mad!

Do not stomp.
Do not shout.

Breathe in.
Breathe out.

Slowly count
from one to ten.

Do it again.
Do it again.

Ziggy! Do you hear that beat?

Yes! I will follow my feet!

Join the party, everyone. . . .

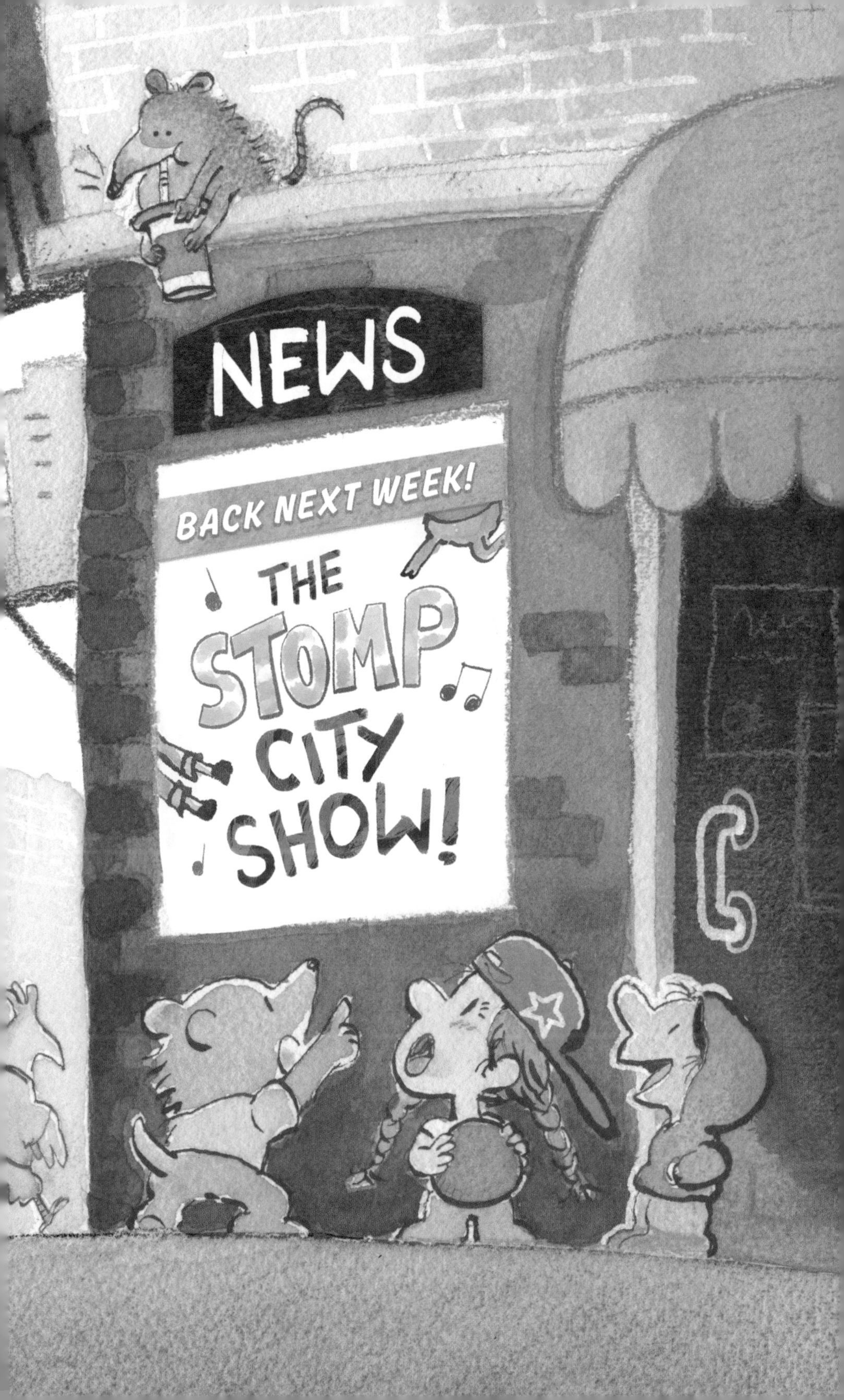
NEWS
BACK NEXT WEEK!
THE STOMP CITY SHOW!

Now that you have read the story, can you answer these questions?

1. Why are Ziggy and Zak running late for the show? How would you feel if you were running late for a show?

2. When Ziggy is upset, what does he do to feel better?

3. In this story you read the rhyming words "flat" and "that." Can you think of other words that rhyme with "flat" and "that"?

Great job!

You are a reading star!